ME AND MY AUNTS

Laura P. Newton
pictures by Robin Oz

Albert Whitman & Company, Niles, Illinois

J
N

Text © 1986 by Laura P. Newton.
Illustrations © 1986 by Robin Oz.
Published in 1986 by Albert Whitman & Company, Niles, Illinois.
Published simultaneously in Canada by
General Publishing, Limited, Toronto.
All rights reserved. Printed in the U.S.A.
10 9 8 7 6 5 4 3 2 1

Library of Congress Cataloging-in-Publication Data

Newton, Laura P.
  Me and my aunts.

  Summary: A little girl loves all her talented
aunts, though her favorite is one who doesn't bake
or sew or travel, but instead remembers how it
feels to be a child.
  [1. Aunts—Fiction] I. Oz, Robin, ill. II. Title
PZ7.N4868Me 1986   [Fic]   86-15950
ISBN 0-8075-5029-9

For Helene, Lee, Patricia,
and all the aunts who remember L. N.
For Cody and Frank R. O.

I have lots and lots of relatives.
Best of all are my aunts.

One aunt is the best baker in the world.
She makes pies and cookies and fancy cakes,
even when it's not my birthday.
I love to visit her.

One aunt is a champion at sewing.
She makes me pretty pillows for my bed,
toasty sweaters that are easy to put on,
and long, pink lacy dresses that
my mother would never pick out.

One aunt is a teacher.
She is very smart.
She brings me important books
that I will enjoy . . . next year.

One aunt is a great traveler.
She sends me gifts from all over the world.
This year she's going to China.

My most favorite aunt can't bake.
She *hates* to sew.
She doesn't teach,
and she travels only to see me.
She is a Rememberer.

She remembers that it's scary when you wake up
in the middle of the night and there's thunder.

She remembers how it is when you don't have a best friend.

She remembers what it's like to have a pesky little brother.

She remembers that hot, heavy feeling
when you break something by accident.

She remembers to take an extra apple
on a hike in case we meet a unicorn,

to bring a mirror when my hair is white with shampoo,
so I can see how I'll look when I'm very, very old,

to make popcorn on a rainy day, for no good reason at all,

to wake me up so we can watch the new day borning.

I am learning to bake,
and I can sew, a little.
I might be a teacher,
and I'd surely like to travel.

But when I am an aunt,
most of all,

I will remember.